8/16

THE
SLEEPING PORCH

by Karen Ackerman • illustrated by Elizabeth Sayles

Morrow Junior Books / New York

Pastels were used for the full-color illustrations.
The text type is 18-point Couchin Bold.

Printed in the United States of America.

1 2 3 4 5 6 7 8 9 10

Library of Congress Cataloging-in-Publication Data
Ackerman, Karen.
The sleeping porch / by Karen Ackerman; illustrated by Elizabeth Sayles.
p. cm.
Summary: A rainstorm sends a family from their long-awaited first house, with all of its leaks,
onto the sleeping porch to enjoy the pleasures of the summer night.
ISBN 0-688-12822-X (trade) — ISBN 0-688-12823-8 (library)
[1. Porches—Fiction.   2. Dwellings—Fiction.   3. Moving, Household—Fiction.]
I. Sayles, Elizabeth, ill.   II. Title.   PZ7.A1824Sl 1995   [E]—dc20   94-16645   CIP AC

For my friend Natalie King, with love.
—K.A.

For Jessica, welcome to the world!
—E.S.

*L*ast year our parents bought their very first house. My younger brothers, Mitch and Hal, and sisters, Becca and Lilly, still had to share bedrooms and closets, but they were excited anyway. As the oldest, I got a bedroom all to myself, which I thought was great. But none of us imagined how much trouble the house would turn out to be.

We lived in a small apartment, and sometimes our parents got cranky because we were always bumping into each other in the halls and doorways.

"I feel like I'm living in a Cracker Jack box!" Mom would groan, usually when she was trying to find room to put something away—and there *wasn't* any room. "Won't we ever have a house of our own?" she'd ask Dad.

Dad would laugh and say, "I should've been born a Rock-a-fella!" and though we didn't know exactly what a rock-a-fella was, we laughed too because it sounded funny.

Then one day Mom and Dad told us that they'd bought a house. We all begged to see it, and Dad said, "Let's take them on a pass-by," so we piled into the car.

When Dad stopped in front of the house, we thought we were dreaming. It was bigger than any of us could believe, though it needed some paint and fixing up.

"You'll finally have your own room, Jonathan," Mom said to me. "And there's a sleeping porch!"

"What's that, Mom?" Mitch asked from the backseat.

"See over on the right? It's built on the side of the house and all screened in," she answered. "When I was a girl, our house had one too."

The day we moved in, Mom sighed, "This is the happiest day of my life!" and we felt the same way.

Mitch and Hal started to stuff things in their closet and thumbtack kung-fu posters up on the walls. Becca and Lilly unpacked dolls and stuffed animals and lined them on their twin beds.

Mom covered the kitchen-cabinet shelves with paper and unpacked dishes, pots, and pans.

"C'mon, Jonathan," Dad said to me, and I helped him carry the storage boxes into the basement and garage.

By the time most of the packing boxes were emptied, we were starting to feel at home in our new house.

Then one hot summer night there was a terrible thunderstorm, and all the lights went out.

"It's okay," Dad reassured us, and he got out his flashlight while Mom lit a few candles.

But then we heard a dripping sound—*everywhere*. Water suddenly poured through the roof into the bedrooms, dining room, family room, kitchen, and bathrooms.

Mom rushed to get pots and pans from the kitchen and told us to put them under the drips. Dad tried to stop the leaks with duct tape, and the rest of us ran around in the candlelight, searching for drips.

But there were too many, and we gave up, laughing, playing in the raindrop waterfall and having splash fights. The thunder was so loud that Lilly started to cry, and Becca crawled under the dining-room table. We huddled together with candles and Dad's flashlight till the storm was over.

There wasn't a dry place left inside. The bedroom carpets were soaked, the kitchen floor was flooded, and the dining-room walls were streaked from dripping water.

"Now what?" Dad moaned, looking at the ruined carpets and walls. "Where are we going to sleep?"

"How about the sleeping porch?" Mom softly asked.

So we got some pillows, sheets, and light summer blankets from the upstairs linen closet, and we followed Mom down the hallway, where Dad waited with an armful of pillows and bed sheets from their room. Then we all trailed out to the sleeping porch in one long line of cranky, unhappy people in damp pj's.

The air was so steamy that it was almost hard to breathe—but suddenly a breeze came through the screens like someone softly blowing on the backs of our necks. The wind chimes tinkled, the stars twinkled, and everything smelled fresh and green like a forest.

Mom helped us fold the blankets into sleeping bags, tucked the sheets in and under with the pillows on top, and put the blanket bags together in a circle, heads in and feet out like the spokes of a wagon wheel.

Dad lit some citronella candles because mosquitoes were getting in through a few holes in the screens, and the smell of lemons and candle wax filled our noses.

Crickets sang a dancing, snappy-castanet song, and june bugs buzzed at the screens. Everyone settled down, listening to the night music and watching fireflies.

"This is great!" I whispered to Dad, and he smiled for the first time all night. He and Mom chuckled as they arranged their elbows and knees to snuggle together in their blanket bags.

"It's just like I remember, Dan," Mom sighed to Dad. "Isn't this wonderful?"

I heard him say "Um-hum" before I fell asleep.

Since then, the leaky roof has been fixed, and the sleeping porch gets used for a lot of things.

In the fall Dad and I set up a folding table and help Mitch, Hal, Becca, and Lilly carve pumpkins. On Halloween the sleeping porch is full of funny-faced jack-o'-lanterns with candles burning inside.

In the winter we pile our sleds and boots in a corner near the door. Hats, gloves, and scarves go in a crate marked IDAHO SPUDS that Mom got from Meyer's Grocery. All winter I help Becca and Lilly in and out of their snowsuits and remind Mitch and Hal not to track snow in on the brand-new carpets.

In the spring Mom sets up rows and rows of seedlings in little pots for her summer garden. A few weeks later the sleeping porch is full of tiny flowering buds in a zillion colors, ready for all of us to help Mom plant one afternoon in May.

But in the summer there's always a hot and stormy night when we're sitting around listening to the rain and thunder outside, and one of us just has to ask, "How about the sleeping porch?"

So even though the roof doesn't leak anymore, we'll get our sheets and blankets and pillows, and out we'll march in one long line of happy people in pj's.

And we'll settle down for the night in our very special place, the sleeping porch.